# Christopher Churchmouse Classics™

# THE WHITE TRAIL

*"Let him that stole steal no more"* — *Ephesians 4:28.*

D1537332

## WRITTEN BY BARBARA DAVOLL
### Pictures by Dennis Hockerman

**Chariot**VICTOR
**PUBLISHING**
A DIVISION OF COOK COMMUNICATIONS

Chariot Books is an imprint of ChariotVictor Publishing,
a division of Cook Communications, Colorado Springs, Colorado 80918
Cook Communications, Paris, Ontario
Kingsway Communications, Eastbourne, England

# A WORD TO PARENTS AND TEACHERS

The Christopher Churchmouse Classics will please both the eyes and ears of children, and help them grow in the knowledge of God.

This book, *The White Trail,* one of the character-building stories in the series, is about stealing. Christopher and his friend discover a valuable lesson when an escapade in the church kitchen becomes a nightmare for the young mice. The "white trail" leads right to them as the culprits and also leads them to learn the truth about stealing.

> *"Let him that stole steal no more"*
> —Ephesians 4:28.

Use the Discussion Starters on page 24 to help children make practical application of the biblical truth. Happy reading!

Christopher's Friend,

*Barbara Davoll*

Christopher Churchmouse and his best friend Freddie Fieldmouse waited patiently behind the door of the church kitchen for darkness to come.

"It's almost dark," whispered Freddie nervously to Christopher.

"Yes, we can leave in just a minute," answered Christopher.

"How will we carry the food back to our homes?" asked Freddie.

"We won't," said Christopher. "We'll just eat what we want in the kitchen. Then nobody will ever know we took it."

"Oh," replied Freddie. "I thought we were going to get some to eat later."

"Naw, that's too risky. If my mama and papa knew what I was doing, they would be very angry. I don't dare take any home. Come on, it's dark enough now," said Christopher, stepping cautiously from behind the door. "Follow me."

The mice scampered silently into the big church kitchen.

"Come on over this way to the cupboards," whispered Christopher. "That's where the goodies are."

"What if Tuffy hears us?" Freddie asked anxiously.

"Aw, I can take care of that cat!" Christopher said boldly.

"How will we get the food?"

"You worry too much, Freddie," said Christopher impatiently. "I told you I know the ropes. Just watch me." And Christopher jumped up on the handle of the big cabinet's bottom drawer. "Hop up here like this." Soon he was on top of the counter. "The food is in that top cabinet. All we have to do is push here and presto—the door opens. Come on, give me a boost," demanded Christopher.

By standing on Freddie's shoulders Christopher could reach the top cabinet. Then he pulled Freddie up. "Now for the goodies," squealed Christopher.

"Wow! What's in all these canisters?" asked Freddie.

"Well, this one has oatmeal, and this one has rice, and this one has sugar—good, sticky, sweet stuff. Come on, let's get these lids off."

"Hey, Christopher, this stuff is good," squeaked Freddie, taking a big pawful of oatmeal.

"I know. Wait till you try this brown sugar. It's yummy."

"Aw, it's too bad we can't take some home with us," said Freddie.

"Yeah, but we can come back anytime we want."

"Um-hum," said Freddie with his mouth so full he couldn't talk.

Finally Christopher said, "I'm full. We'd better be getting home. Help me put these lids on."

"Why do we need to put the lids back?" asked Freddie. "Let's just go."

"No, no, Freddie!" exclaimed Christopher. "You put all the lids back so nobody will know we were here."

"OK," agreed Freddie.

Soon the last lid was on. Then just as the mice were ready to hop out of the cabinet, Freddie knocked over the canister of flour, spilling it on the counter. In trying to catch his balance, Freddie tumbled right into the big hill of flour.

"Help, Christopher! I can't breathe!" screamed Freddie, who looked like a white lump.

8

"I'm coming," yelled Christopher, as he jumped down. "Boy, are you a mess!" he said, pulling his friend out of the flour.

"I know that!" said Freddie, coughing and sputtering.

"Well, there's no way to keep anybody from knowing we've been here," said Christopher, as he tried to brush flour off Freddie. "Let's get home as fast as we can."

By this time Christopher was covered with flour too.

"O Chris, you look funny," Freddie said with a laugh. "You look like a white mouse."

"You don't look any different," said Christopher. "Come on, hurry!"

10

Together the mice jumped down
and ran to Christopher's home.

"We'd better get rid of this flour,"
whispered Christopher, taking his
mother's whisk broom from the closet.

"Yeah, you brush me off and I'll
brush you off."

So Christopher turned around
and around as Freddie brushed him,
and he did the same for Freddie.

"There! Now you are a gray
mouse again."

"Yes, and I'd better get home
fast," Freddie said, heading
for the door.

11

The next morning Christopher was still sleeping when Mama called, "Christopher, wake up. Please wake up quickly!"

"What's wrong, Mama?" asked Christopher, sleepily rubbing his eyes.

"O Christopher, after your papa left for work this morning, someone set a trap."

"What?"

"The janitor set a trap right outside our front door."

"Wh—why would he do that?" stammered Christopher.

"I don't know, but we have to warn Papa. He'll walk around the corner and right into that trap for sure," said Mama anxiously.

Jumping out of bed, Christopher said, "I'll get Freddie, and he and I will see what we can find out."

"Please be careful, Son."

"I will, Mama."

Later Christopher and Freddie peered around the corner. The trap was huge! The bait was a piece of yellow cheese.

"Wow! Look at that hunk of cheese," said Freddie.

"Yes," answered Christopher, "and look at that trap. Freddie, that trap could kill my papa!"

"I know. But why would the janitor put it in front of your house?"

"I don't know," said Christopher.

Just then the mice heard a noise and scampered off to hide in the janitor's closet. Soon they heard him come into the closet. Tuffy the cat was at his heels.

"Well, Tuffy," said the janitor, "we've got the mice cornered. Yep, that white trail of flour led right to their doorstep. Now all we've got to do is wait for them to fall into our trap and we'll be rid of them."

Christopher and Freddie froze in horror. The janitor left the closet humming a tune. Tuffy followed him.

"Christopher," said Freddie, "the flour! The flour led him to your door."

"Yes, Freddie. It's all my fault. How am I going to protect my family from the trap?" he cried.

"I'll tell you what," suggested Freddie. "You take one corner of the church and I'll take the other and we'll watch for your father to come home. Then we'll see him, whichever way he comes, and warn him."

"Yes, but Papa will have to know why the trap is there, and I'll have to tell him. I can't lie to him."

"I guess not," Freddie agreed. "Well, anyway, at least we can keep him from getting caught in the trap. Let's go."

14

The mice slithered underneath the janitor's closet door and went to their lookout posts. It was a long, tiresome wait before Christopher saw his papa coming down one of the long halls of the church.

"Pssst, Papa, over here. Over here!" whispered Christopher.

Papa came to the door where Christopher was hiding. "Son, what are you doing here?" asked Papa.

"Papa, I have something to tell you. I wanted to catch you before you got home because there is a trap right outside our door. Mama and I were afraid you would walk right into it."

"Oh my!" exclaimed Papa. "I'm glad you told me, but why is the trap there? The janitor knows we're honest mice, and don't take anything except leftovers."

"Well, Papa, um—well," stammered the guilty little mouse.

"What is it, Christopher?"

"Well, sometimes at night Freddie and I go to the kitchen and take stuff."

The shocked look on Christopher's father's face made Christopher hang his head. "O Papa, I'm sorry, but all we did was get into those canisters and eat some sugar and oatmeal and stuff. We didn't bring anything home and we always put the lids on so things wouldn't spoil."

"Why, Son? Didn't you know

18

that was stealing?"

"Well, yes. I mean no, Papa. I—I don't know. I didn't think it was stealing because we didn't take anything and keep it. All we did was eat it there. Besides, we were hungry."

"Doesn't your Mama cook a delicious supper every evening, and don't you eat till you're full?"

"Yes, Papa."

Christopher was so embarrassed and ashamed. Suddenly he realized he was a thief.

"How did the janitor know you had been stealing?" asked Papa.

"Well, last night Freddie spilled the flour. Then we both got covered with it."

"O Christopher," groaned Papa.

"We brushed ourselves, but we couldn't get it all off. This morning we heard the janitor say that a white trail led right to our door."

And with that Christopher began to cry and sob as if his heart would break. "O Papa, I'm so sorry. Now all the church mice are in danger."

"Yes, we'll all have to stay inside until the janitor takes the trap away. It s just too dangerous to let any of the little children out to play. They would get caught for sure.

"Christopher, you know too that stealing is wrong. I heard the pastor say that one of God's Laws is, 'You shall not steal.' The pastor said those words are in the Bible.

"We're supposed to work for what we have. There are always plenty of crumbs and bits of food for us here in the church. We don't need to become thieves."

"O Papa, I've made a terrible mess, haven't I?"

"Yes, you have, Son. You've caused the janitor to mistrust all of us just because you and Freddie stole."

"I am sorry, Papa."

Later that night, Christopher was sitting in the living room with Mama and Papa.

"Christopher," said Papa, "I've been thinking what would be the best way to correct you for your disobedience. Remember, God's Word tells people, 'Let him that stole steal no more: but rather let him labor, working with his hands.'

21

"Those words give me an idea, Christopher. Because you are the cause of the trap, I believe you should be the one to work and bring food to us. You can go out the back way. Take your wagon and bring home whatever crumbs you find. Maybe working for the food will help you remember not to steal."

"How long will they leave that trap out there?" asked Christopher.

"I don't know," said Papa. "It could be quite a while."

The trap was there for a whole week, and during that time Christopher brought food to his family every day.

You can be sure Christopher had learned his lesson and never again stole from the church kitchen or anywhere else.

## DISCUSSION STARTERS

1. Where did Christopher and his friend get into trouble?
2. Do you think the two mice meant to steal?
3. How were they found out?
4. What was outside Christopher's door the next morning?
5. When we do wrong, are we usually the only ones to be hurt?
6. What lesson did you learn from this story about stealing? What should you do if you have stolen something?

Ask the Lord to help you never to steal.